Contents

Chapter 1   A Family with Problems

Sandy Stern had been married to his wife Clara for thirty-one years and he thought he knew her well. But when he returned home from Chicago one afternoon in March he began to realize that he understood very little about her.

He had been in Chicago for two days and before he left everything seemed fine. Now, as he stood at the front door of the house he and Clara had shared for about twenty years he knew immediately something was wrong. It was very quiet, no sound from the radio, no taps running. He called Clara's name but there was no answer.

He found her in the garage. She was sitting in the driver's seat of her car with the engine running and the garage door closed. Her head lay back against the seat with her eyes closed and her mouth open. She had no jacket or handbag with her. He had no doubt that she was dead.

Sandy made two phone calls, first to the police then to his son Peter who was a doctor in the same town.

'Something is wrong with Mother,' said Peter at once and Sandy told him to come home immediately.

Very soon, the house was full of strangers, police and ambulance men. Outside, the neighbours were watching what was happening. Peter arrived quickly and went to the garage after speaking to his father. The police started to ask Sandy about Clara.

'Was your wife usually a happy woman?'

'She was a serious person. She was very private.'

'Had she ever said she might do this?'

'No, never.'

'Why did you go to Chicago?'

Sandy told them about his trip, that he was Dixon Hartnell's lawyer, and he sometimes went to Chicago because of him. Dixon

1

was married to Sandy's sister Silvia and he was a very rich businessman. He owned a big company called Maison Dixon, or MD, which bought and sold a lot of different things and he was often in trouble with government officials. Recently the FBI★ had given subpoenas to some MD customers in Chicago for information about MD and Sandy had gone to talk with their lawyers. Sandy thought it was really Dixon that the FBI were investigating.

Another policeman arrived, someone Sandy knew a little. His name was Ray Radczyk. He asked Sandy about Clara's health, and more about his trip to Chicago.

Suddenly, a policeman said they had found something in the bedroom. It was a note for Sandy but it was very short. There were only four words, 'Can you forgive me?'

♦

Sandy woke up early on the day of Clara's funeral and it was still dark. His older daughter Marta was still asleep in her room. She was a lawyer in New York and had come home as soon as he had telephoned her. His younger daughter Kate and her husband John had also stayed at the house although they lived in the same town. Sandy's sister Silvia was there as well but Dixon was away somewhere on business. Peter was at his flat.

Sandy dressed and went to the kitchen. He couldn't understand why Clara had killed herself or how he hadn't seen that something was wrong. He made coffee and found a lot of letters on the table that were addressed to Clara. He hadn't opened any of them. He looked through them and found one with Westlab Hospital on the envelope. Inside was a bill for a doctor's test but he didn't know what it was for. As he sat and looked at it Kate came downstairs.

She was tall and beautiful with long dark hair.

She had met John at High School, a kind and gentle boy who

★ Federal Bureau of Investigation: the USA's national crime fighting body.

Suddenly, a policeman said they had found something in the bedroom.

had been an excellent football player but a poor student. After university they got married and Dixon gave John a job at MD. He still worked for him.

Kate touched her father's hand.

'Daddy I want you to know something. We're going to have a baby.'

Sandy was very happy for Kate and he kissed her. Marta came down then and Kate told her. Like Sandy, Marta was short and a little fat and she had a lot of black hair and glasses. The sisters looked very different but they were good friends. Marta was delighted about the baby.

Peter arrived at the house and then later, Dixon. Away from the rest of the family, Dixon asked Sandy what he had learned in Chicago.

'There may be a problem, Dixon. We'll talk about it later.'

Dixon had started smoking again, a sign that he was worried. Silvia told him about the baby and he put his arm around Kate but she moved away from him. The children had never liked Dixon much although they loved their Aunt Silvia. Everyone knew he had other women and that his business was not always completely honest but he was John's boss and one of the family.

Just as the funeral cars arrived two men came to the house to see Dixon. Sandy thought they were people from MD who needed to talk about work, but one of them gave Dixon some papers and then he started shouting at them. Sandy took the papers from Dixon and realized that the men were FBI detectives and they had just given Dixon a subpoena. He was very annoyed.

'We're going to a funeral,' he said. 'My wife's. It's a very sad day for my family. You can't do this now.'

The FBI men took the papers back.

'Monday, your office, nine o'clock,' said one of them to Dixon. Then they left and the family went together to Clara Stern's funeral.

♦

When Sandy arrived at his office on Tuesday, Dixon was already there. The subpoena had come the day before and now they had to decide what to do next.

'So, Dixon, what's all this about?'

'I'm not sure. Is it me they're investigating?'

Sandy thought it was. The subpoena asked for some papers but he thought that was just the beginning and the FBI would soon want more. The US Government would possibly try to prosecute Dixon eventually if they could find enough proof. Sandy was worried about another thing, too.

'One other thing, Dixon. Why has the government started this now? Somebody is giving them information and we must find out who it is. Have you any ideas?'

Dixon didn't know who it could be. They read the subpoena again. Dixon had to give the FBI a lot of papers for different customers and dates and Sandy asked him to explain them.

'This first one, Chicago Ovens. They make nearly half the cakes sold in supermarkets. Sugar was selling at a good price in July. They wanted to be certain they could buy it at a good price in December so we bought it for them in July to deliver in December. At MD we wrote that on our order desk in the offices here and sent it to the right market to buy – this went to Chicago. There we found someone who wanted to sell December sugar. Next day we got the money from the customer, Chicago Ovens. The FBI want all the pieces of paper from this sale.'

Sandy looked at the subpoena again.

'And these other companies, are they the same?'

'Yes, but they're all buying different things. They're my five biggest customers and these are all very big sales. That sometimes makes the price at the market change.'

'So, the government is looking at large sales with MD. The ones that can change the market prices.'

Sandy telephoned the US Government Lawyer's office and spoke to Sonia Klonsky, who had signed the subpoena.

'Ms Klonsky, what exactly are you investigating?'

'I can't answer.'

'Is it Mr Hartnell?'

'I can't say. Those papers should be here today.'

'Mr Hartnell has a very big business and there are a lot of papers to look for. We need more time.'

'How long?'

'Another four weeks.'

Sonia Klonsky wasn't happy, but she agreed.

'OK Mr Stern, May 2nd. I'll send you a letter. Then we'll meet after I've read the papers.'

Sandy put the phone down. He told Dixon to be very careful and not to speak to anyone at all about what had happened.

'Remember, someone is giving the FBI information and we don't know who it is.'

Dixon left Sandy's office looking worried.

Sandy remembered speaking to Clara once about Dixon. She had never liked him much. Sandy had said that he thought Dixon was a difficult man to understand completely and Clara had answered: 'He probably says the same of you.'

Chapter 2   Mysteries

A week after the funeral Sandy and his children visited Clara's lawyer. Her parents had been very rich and when they died they left their money to Clara. Now the family had come to find out who Clara had arranged to leave the money to.

The lawyer explained that she wanted to give some money to the church and there was some for the children. They were each going to receive $200,000. The rest was for Sandy and the lawyer explained that it added up to $850,000. Then he asked Sandy what had happened to that money.

Sandy didn't understand.

The lawyer asked Sandy what had happened to that money.
Sandy didn't understand.

'It's gone,' said the lawyer.

It was silent in the room for a moment. No one knew what to say. Then Sandy spoke again.

'Do you mean someone has stolen it?'

'No, nothing like that. But Clara took $850,000 from her bank account five days before she died,' said the lawyer. 'I thought you must know what she did with it. Didn't you discuss it with her?'

Sandy didn't know what Clara had done with the money or where it had gone. Neither he nor the children could guess and they were all very surprised.

'What would Mother do with $850,000? It's a lot of money,' said Marta.

'I thought perhaps she bought a summer house, something like that, and I wanted to ask you first,' said the lawyer. 'But now that I can see that you don't know, I'll phone the bank. Don't worry, we'll find it.'

Sandy didn't need the money, but Clara hadn't discussed it with him and it seemed very strange.

Kate started crying and Peter put his arm round her. The family left the office together. Nobody could guess what had happened to so much money. It was another thing Sandy didn't understand about his wife.

◆

Quite soon after Clara's funeral, Sandy went back to his office and started working again. The other lawyers who worked for him had looked after most things, but Sandy wanted to work on Dixon's problems personally.

One day Dixon phoned him at the office and told him that the FBI had given subpoenas to more of his customers and also to the manager of his personal bank. This was where Dixon kept his own money, not the company's money.

'What does it mean?' he asked Sandy.

'It means the FBI are certainly investigating you, Dixon. And they think you have personally made money from the big sales we talked about the other day. Perhaps someone paid you for information about sales that would change the market prices. If they knew about it before it happened it would be possible for them to make a profit.'

'But I'm not stupid. If I took money like that I wouldn't put it in my cheque account. It's too obvious.'

There was something about Dixon's voice that told Sandy he was frightened.

'The FBI are also looking at the computer figures for one of the MD accounts,' he told Sandy.

'Which one?'

'The house error account.'

Sandy asked Dixon what that was and he explained that it was used when there was a mistake at MD. If the company bought the wrong things for a customer it would pay for them with money in the house error account, then sell them to another customer later.

Sandy told Dixon the FBI could subpoena him as well, and Dixon became more worried.

'I have some personal things in a locked safe and I don't want the FBI to get them. It's in my office. Maybe I should take it home.'

'The FBI might want to search your office but if they don't find what they are looking for they might go to your home next. If that worries you, you should move the safe somewhere they won't look.'

Sandy told Dixon to bring the safe to his office because the FBI probably wouldn't be able to look there for it. He said he would give Dixon a key to the office so that he could get to the safe whenever he wanted to.

'You must arrange it yourself, Dixon. Only you and I should know where the safe is.'

Sandy reminded Dixon to be very careful who he talked to about it. They still didn't know who the FBI were getting information from.

'It must be someone close to you or the business,' he said. 'All the information the FBI are getting is correct.'

♦

One evening, about five weeks after Clara had died, Sandy had a phone call from Helen Dudak. She was an old friend of Sandy and Clara's and her daughter had been Kate's best friend at school. Helen's husband had died about three years ago.

She told Sandy she would bring him some dinner. It was a kind thought, typical of Helen.

Sandy liked Helen. She was about his age, amusing and attractive. She had cooked him some chicken and there was enough for two so she stayed for dinner and Sandy opened a bottle of wine.

While they were eating, Sandy's next door neighbour Nate Cawley called. Nate was a doctor and he had sometimes looked after Clara although he didn't usually ask her to pay him. Sandy had left a message for Nate to call because he wanted to ask him about the bill from Westlab Hospital. He thought perhaps Nate had told Clara to have the test because he hadn't found a doctor's bill.

'Was she ill, Nate? Something serious, I mean.'

'Nothing I know about. I could phone the hospital for you, try to find out? Sometimes things get mixed up. It might be a bill for another Stern.'

After Nate had left, Sandy suddenly thought he understood. Clara was probably paying for a test Kate had for the baby.

'Yes,' said Helen. 'That must be the answer.'

They talked about Clara. He said, 'I have no idea why she killed herself'

'You must be very angry,' answered Helen.

'Angry, yes, but more than that. I failed. I couldn't see what was wrong.'

'Maybe Clara failed as well.'

Sandy didn't answer.

'You must try to remember things before the end. You were a wonderful couple, Sandy.

'You're a real friend Helen. And it's good to talk to you.'

After that they both talked about their children and Sandy said all his family were very pleased about Kate and John's baby.

They had a pleasant evening together and talked a lot. They agreed to meet again another time and when Helen said goodbye, Sandy kissed her hand.

A few days later, Sandy visited Kate and John at their house. They were a very happy couple and he was pleased to be with them for an evening. Sandy and John watched a football match on the television. They didn't talk much, but John was always quiet. He was quite different to Sandy's family, who were all clever and good at music. But he was a kind husband and he and Kate loved each other very much.

Sandy never asked John about work. He knew that John didn't like to talk to him about it because he thought Sandy might repeat anything he said to Dixon. John had had a slow start at MD. It was difficult for him to work with computers or accounts and eventually Dixon had given him a job on the order desk. Sandy thought it was probably boring work, but John continued to work there.

After the football had finished, when Sandy was in the kitchen with Kate, he asked her about the bill from Westlab Hospital.

'Mother didn't pay for any tests for me, Daddy.'

'Oh well, it's nothing,' he said. But then he suddenly had another idea. Peter was a doctor and he wouldn't give his mother a bill if he advised her to have the test.

'Did she ever go to see Peter as a doctor?'

Kate looked very surprised and he decided not to say any more. It was obvious she thought he was silly to worry about something like that.

'Daddy, are you OK?'

'Yes, yes. It's not important. Forget it.'

He said goodbye to Kate and John and drove home. But he didn't forget about the hospital test.

Clara had left him with so many mysteries.

Chapter 3   Cheating

Soon after the evening Sandy had spent with Kate and John, Sandy travelled to Chicago from his home in Kindle. He had to go to MD there to study the papers Sonia Klonsky wanted to see before they were sent to her. One of the secretaries had brought him some boxes full of papers and he started looking through them, but he was confused by the figures.

All round him people working at MD's Chicago office rushed from room to room and the phones were never quiet. In the enormous room next to the office where Sandy was sitting were about eighty young men and women, each working in front of a computer and telephone. It was all very different to his own peaceful office.

He looked at the papers in front of him and tried reading them again but then he heard a voice from the office door.

'So, do you understand it all now, Sandy?'

It was Margy Allison, Dixon's chief manager in Chicago. Sandy looked up at her.

'I think I need a little help, actually.'

She laughed. Sandy had known Margy for many years and they were friends. She had worked at MD since leaving university nearly twenty years before. She had started working for Dixon as a secretary and now she had reached the top. Margy knew everything about MD's accounts and she was the right person to help Sandy understand them.

'But it will take a lot of time and you're always so busy here,' he said.

'No problem, Sandy. Are you staying in Chicago tonight? We could look at the accounts this evening, if you like. You can buy me dinner.'

Margy was attractive and dressed very well and Sandy had often thought that she was one of Dixon's women. About seven years ago Silvia had made Dixon leave their home for several weeks and he had thought at the time it was because of Margy. But MD in Chicago couldn't operate without her at the top and so she had stayed in her job and eventually Dixon had gone back to live with Silvia. Dixon had never said anything about it to Sandy so he didn't know if he was right about Margy.

They agreed it was a good idea to look at the papers together that evening.

'Is the house error account here Margy?'

'They want that now, too?' she replied and sent someone to get another box. Later they took them all to Sandy's hotel and started to look at them together.

Margy explained a lot about the figures to Sandy and they tried to understand why the government lawyers had subpoenaed only certain papers. There didn't seem to be any special plan. But then Margy had an idea and started checking the papers again. She realized what Dixon was doing.

'He's cheating the markets,' she said.

'And making a big profit?'

'Yes, but Dixon's clever. He hides the money in the house error account. He makes it look just like a mistake with a customer's sale so nobody knows what he's doing.'

They looked at the figures again and Sandy started to understand.

'So when he telephones the people on the order desk they do what he says and they don't think it's strange?' he asked.

'No. He telephones them hundreds of times every week. If it sounded like an ordinary sale nobody would think it was any different. They wouldn't even remember.'

'They won't catch him. There's nothing here with his name on it.
But that's what he's doing.'

Margy smiled at Sandy.

'They won't catch him. There's nothing here with his name on it. But that's what he's doing.'

◆

Sandy's flight from Chicago back to his home in Kindle was delayed. He had a long time to wait at the airport and so he called Ray Radczyk at the police office.

'I was just wondering whether the doctor's report on my wife's death said anything unusual?'

'It was only a short examination, Sandy. They tested her blood for CO* poisoning and agreed she had killed herself. That's all. Why do you ask?'

Sandy told him about the Westlab Hospital bill.

'I could go to the hospital and find out, if you like. I'll go myself and get the information.'

Sandy was grateful to Radczyk, but he also felt worried about what he might find.

◆

On the next Friday, Sandy took all the papers subpoenaed from MD to Sonia Klonsky's office. It was the first time he had met her and he was surprised to see that, like Kate, she was going to have a baby. But Ms Klonsky was much older than Kate, about forty Sandy guessed. She was short and dark-haired, an attractive woman with large eyes. He congratulated her and told her his daughter was also going to have a baby. She asked about Kate's health, then said she was sorry about Clara. It was about six weeks since she had died and people still spoke about it.

Sandy gave her the papers.

'Can you tell me what you're looking for?'

'Sorry, Sandy, I can't.'

* Carbon monoxide: A gas that comes from car engines and can poison you.

15

'Is there an informant?'

'If there is, I don't know who it is. Does it matter if someone is giving us information?'

'I think Mr Hartnell should know what is being said against him. If he knew, we may be able to help more.'

Sonia Klonsky continued taking the papers out of the boxes.

'There'll be subpoenas going to certain people from MD soon and they'll have to have different lawyers. You couldn't work for Mr Hartnell and for them, I'm sure you understand that.'

Sandy could tell something new was coming and he guessed it was going to be bad.

'Anyway Sandy, I thought it was better to give this one to you personally. He's got a month before we want to see him so there's plenty of time for you to help him find a lawyer.'

She gave Sandy a single piece of paper. On the front was typed the name John Granum, Kate's husband.

'Will you be seeing other people from the order desk?' he asked, but Sonia said no, just John.

'Could he be immune? Is that a possibility?'

'Yes. If he tells us what we want to know, we won't prosecute him. I'm sorry about this, Sandy.'

He took John's subpoena and left her office feeling worried and unhappy. It seemed his family troubles were getting worse and he was angry with Dixon for causing problems for John.

◆

Sandy had arranged to meet Radczyk in a bar by the river. When he arrived the policeman was already there. He took a paper from his jacket.

'Have you talked to her doctors?' asked Radczyk.

Sandy explained that he had spoken to Nate, but he didn't know anything about the test.

Radczyk looked at the paper.

16

'No name here. This is a copy of the test results.' He gave it to Sandy. There was nothing on it he could understand.

'Did they say what the test was for?'

'Yes, a virus. Here – HSV–2.'

'And did my wife have the virus?'

'Sandy, maybe I ought to go back and get that doctor's name for you.'

Sandy knew something was wrong.

'Did she have the virus?'

Radczyk nodded.

'And what is this virus?'

Radczyk looked uncomfortable.

'I think the doctor should tell you that.'

'I see. Are you refusing to tell me?'

'No, I'll tell you. I asked the lady at the hospital and this is what she told me. It was a test for herpes.'

Sandy was shocked. His wife had a virus that she could only have got by having sex with someone who already had it. He heard Radczyk talking again.

'. . . know any details. I'm going back to the hospital now to find out who the doctor was. I think you ought to talk to him.'

'No, no. It's all right. You've done enough.'

Sandy stood up, shook hands with Radczyk and the policeman gave him the paper.

As he walked out of the bar, Sandy wondered where he could go to be alone. My God, Clara, he thought. My God, Clara, why did you do this?

Chapter 4   Getting Advice

After the shock of finding out that Clara had herpes Sandy realized Peter could not have known about it. No mother, he thought, could ask her own son for advice about something like that.

But now Sandy needed Peter's advice. He didn't intend to tell
Peter about Clara, but he needed more information and he wanted
to know if he also had the virus. Sandy and Peter didn't always
understand each other, they were very different people. It had
always been Clara that Peter was close to, not his father. Sandy had
never been to Peter's office before, so when he arrived there Peter
was very surprised to see him.

'What's wrong?' he asked.

'I need some advice, Peter. Something difficult to discuss.'

They went to Peter's room, a typical doctor's office. Sandy
noticed a recent photo of Clara on the desk, and guessed it had only
been there since she died.

'So, what's the problem?'

'I need some information . . .'

'What happened to Nate?'

It was a good question. Sandy had spent the weekend telephon-
ing Nate and leaving messages for him, but he hadn't called back.

'I thought I could ask you . . .'

'Yes, of course, I just wondered. So what is it?'

Sandy told him and said he was asking for a friend who was
worried. He said nothing about Clara. But Peter saw there was
more to it than that.

'Dad, do you think you have herpes?'

'I need to know if it's possible, my friend needs to know . . .'

It was no good. Peter had guessed that Sandy was asking for
himself. Sandy could see he was shocked. His mother had only been
dead two months and now his father was worried that he had
caught herpes from another woman. But he was a good doctor, so
he examined Sandy and took some tests.

'You're probably OK,' he said. 'Some people are naturally
immune anyway. The tests will take about six weeks and then we'll
know for certain.'

Sandy asked him about the virus. Peter told him there were very good pills called Acyclovir that could control it but in some people it returned after about ten days. Sometimes it disappeared for many years and then returned. Sandy had one last question.

'Is it only possible to catch it through sex?'

'Yes. There's no other way.'

♦

Dixon and Sandy met for lunch the next day and discussed Dixon's problems with the government lawyers. Sandy told him he had seen Margy and taken the papers to Sonia Klonsky.

'I looked at them carefully before I gave them to Ms Klonsky.'

'And?'

'And I'm very worried.'

Dixon said nothing and continued eating.

'Dixon, this is very serious you know.'

'You've said that in the past.'

'And I was right, you've been lucky in the past. You might not be this time.'

Dixon didn't answer for a moment. Then he said, 'Did my safe arrive?'

Dixon's locked safe had arrived at Sandy's office the week before. It was heavy and looked very strong.

'You said you'd send me a key to your office.'

'You'll get it soon. Dixon, those papers that I looked at show that someone at MD has made a lot of money in the markets and put it in the house error account. Almost $600,000 profit.'

'So what happens next? They'll want the money back I suppose?'

'That will be the start. They could close MD as well. Then they could put you in prison.'

Dixon was quiet while he thought about it.

'There's no proof it was me. Maybe another person in the office did it and I didn't know about it.'

'They want John to be a witness against you. Does that worry you?'

'Then you and MD would be safe, if that was what really happened. But it's your account, Dixon.'

'It's the house account.'

'It's your house. That's how the government lawyers will see it.'

They continued their lunch in silence. Then Sandy told Dixon that the government had subpoenaed John.

'They have said he might possibly be immune,' he added.

'What are you telling me?' asked Dixon.

'If John tells them what they want to know, they won't prosecute him. They want him to be a witness against you. Does that worry you?'

Dixon had stopped eating.

'Possibly.'

'Then we had better find him another lawyer because I can't advise both you and John. I'll give him a list of names, people I know who are good lawyers.'

'Look . . .' For a moment Sandy thought Dixon was going to explain what had happened and why. But then he seemed to change his mind and started eating again. Sandy could see Dixon had no more to say that day.

◆

Clara's lawyer had asked Sandy to meet him at her bank so they could talk to the manager about the $850,000 that had gone from her account.

The manager had a letter Clara had sent to the bank saying she wanted to arrange for a cheque for $850,000. He said that she came to the bank for the cheque but she didn't write it to herself.

The bank official who had helped Clara with the cheque came into the manager's office.

'Who was the cheque for?' Sandy asked her.

'Nobody has cashed the cheque yet, so we can't look at it,' she replied.

21

'Don't you remember, Ms Fiori? You helped my wife that day.'

Ms Fiori stopped to think.

'I know it wasn't written to Mrs Stern, but I can't remember the name.'

Sandy tried again.

'Was it a company? Or a church or school?'

'No, nothing like that.'

'Just one person, then?'

'Yes, I think so,' she said.

Sandy knew what was coming next.

'A man's name?' he asked.

'Yes,' said Ms Fiori.

For a moment it was quiet in the room, then Sandy spoke again.

'So somewhere a man is walking around with my wife's cheque for $850,000 in his pocket and there is nothing we can do about it?'

It was obvious the bank manager was worried.

'We'll tell you the moment he comes in to cash the cheque, Mr Stern,' he promised.

Outside again in the street, Sandy watched people walking past the bank, men in suits who looked similar to himself. And as he looked at them he wondered, who was it?

◆

Later that week, Sandy went to see John at MD. He explained that the government were investigating Dixon.

'Has anyone from the FBI tried to speak to you?'

John said he didn't think so. Sandy gave him the subpoena and explained what it meant.

'I can't advise you John, because I am already advising Dixon. You must find another lawyer now to talk to. MD will pay for it.'

'Why do they want me?' asked John.

'They want you as a witness against Dixon, but I think you could

22

be immune from prosecution. Your lawyer will explain more about this to you.'

'But what if I don't want to talk?'

'You may have to talk, or go to prison.'

John looked confused.

'I really don't know that much,' he said.

But more than nothing, thought Sandy. John went back to work and Sandy drove home from MD feeling angry with Dixon for bringing so much trouble to his family. Dixon had probably thought John would do anything he told him to and keep quiet, because he was a relation. Sandy knew that was now impossible for John and he could see his whole family separating round him.

First Clara, he thought, and now this.

Chapter 5   Some Papers, Some Questions

Helen Dudak had phoned Sandy to ask him to her house for dinner and he had agreed. Then later, he remembered that Clara had bought two tickets for an evening of music in Kindle the same day. He decided to take Helen there first and eat together afterwards.

Sandy didn't like music much, but Clara had always enjoyed it so they had often gone together to listen. There were a lot of people in the theatre who had known both Sandy and Clara and they waved across at him, but nobody came over to speak to him. He suddenly felt sad and realized his new life had started. But he liked being with Helen and soon found he was enjoying the evening.

Helen cooked a wonderful dinner and they talked about their work and the future.

'There are some good things about being alone again,' said Helen. 'Being free to do the things you want to do, finding yourself.'

Sandy knew she was right. Although he missed Clara a lot he saw that sometimes he enjoyed being selfish again. Perhaps it was a good

They arranged to spend another evening together and
then said goodbye at Helen's door.

thing, he thought, to discover things about himself that he had forgotten.

He knew Helen wanted them to become more than friends but there was too much worrying him at that time. His mind was full of other things, especially the tests Peter had taken for herpes. He still had to wait several weeks for the results. But they arranged to spend another evening together and then said goodbye at Helen's door.

◆

The next morning Margy phoned Sandy at his office. She had received a subpoena from the Chicago FBI and had to bring some papers to Kindle. The date they had given her was June 27th, in three weeks' time.

Sandy asked her to see him before she went to court so that he could look at the papers first. Ms Klonsky wanted to ask her about them and Sandy knew he must tell Margy what questions were likely. Again, the government's informant had been correct. Margy was the person who knew MD's accounts best.

Among the papers the government wanted to talk to Margy about were the tickets from the order desk. Sandy knew some of these were the ones John had written for Dixon. This was the money that had ended up in the house error account. The informant was right again.

Ms Klonsky also wanted to see the papers for something called the Wunderkind account. Sandy asked Margy to explain to him about it.

'I've looked at that. I think it's where Dixon has moved the money to from the error account. I'll find all the details by the 27th.'

Everything was becoming clear. If the government could show that Dixon controlled the Wunderkind account they would have proof that he was cheating the markets. Sandy could see why he was worried.

◆

A letter had arrived from Westlab to remind Clara that she had not paid their bill. Sandy decided he must go to the hospital himself to pay it and while he was there find out which doctor Clara had used.

At the desk inside the hospital doors he found a young lady to ask about it.

'This bill was sent to my wife before she died and I'm afraid I forgot to pay it,' he said.

'That's all right,' she replied. 'No problem.'

He waited for a moment before continuing.

'There was probably a doctor's bill as well, but I can't find it. I'd like to be certain it was paid but I'm not sure who it was. Could you tell me the name of the doctor who ordered the test?'

The girl took Sandy's copy of the bill and disappeared into another room. When she returned she was carrying some other papers and she looked at them for a moment.

'Yes, here it is,' she said. 'Dr Nathaniel Cawley. Would you like his address?'

Nate! Sandy felt suddenly cold. Nate had said he didn't know anything about the Westlab test. Had he lied to Sandy, or had he just forgotten?

Outside the hospital, on his car phone, Sandy telephoned Nate's office.

'I just wanted to ask you something about Clara . . .'

'Is it this Westlab thing again Sandy? I'm sorry I haven't called you but I've been very busy. I checked at Westlab and they couldn't find anything so it must be a mistake. Why don't you just forget it?'

Sandy knew then for certain. Nate was lying. He didn't know why and suddenly he wasn't sure that he wanted to know.

♦

Sandy met Sonia Klonsky outside the court building in Kindle.

'I'd like to talk to you about Margy Allison,' he said. 'I'm going to be her lawyer.'

'Won't that be a problem for you – you're already Mr Hartnell's lawyer?'

They walked together into the building.

'What do you want from her?'

'Some papers, some questions.'

'Is that all you can tell me?'

Ms Klonsky nodded yes, and went into the court. Fifteen minutes later when she came out Sandy was still there, waiting for her.

'Come and have coffee with me,' he said. 'I haven't had breakfast today.'

They went together to a small restaurant near the courts. Sandy waited until they had ordered coffee before asking her what he wanted to know.

'Why are you so interested in the Wunderkind account?'

'Sandy, I can't tell you that.'

'Ms Allison is naturally worried about appearing in court. If she knew exactly what you wanted to know maybe she could help you more.'

'We're not prosecuting her. If she doesn't lie to us she has nothing to worry about. That's all I can say.'

She wouldn't tell him any more so Sandy didn't try to ask her other questions. Instead of that, they talked about his children. He told her that Marta was also a lawyer, working in New York, and Sonia was interested to hear about the work she was doing.

They talked about Sonia's baby. It was her first child but her husband had been married before and had an eight-year-old son called Sam. Sonia was hoping to have a girl and said how much she liked the name Marta. After a time they went back to the courts together.

Sandy liked Sonia and he knew she was a good lawyer. As he watched her walk away into the court he realized Dixon was going to have a long and difficult fight with her.

When Sandy drove back to his house that evening his next door neighbour Fiona, Nate's wife, called to him.

'I've got something to show you,' she said.

He followed her into her house.

'I found this in the bathroom cupboard,' she said. 'It has Clara's name on it.'

She showed him a bag from a chemist's shop. On the ticket, underneath Clara's name where it said 'Doctor', was Nate's name. Sandy looked inside and found a container of pills. The name on the container was Acyclovir. It was the name Peter had told him, the pills for herpes.

'Why are they here if they're Clara's pills?' asked Fiona. Sandy couldn't think of a reply. He put them back where she had found them.

'It's probably nothing important but perhaps you could ask Nate to call me some time,' he said to her.

Back in his own house, he thought about it. Nate had lied to him because he knew Clara had herpes. He had advised her to have the test and he had got her the pills. But why did he keep them in his house? Perhaps, Sandy thought, because Nate was taking the pills, too. Perhaps that was how Clara had caught herpes, from Nate. Then another thought came to him, about the money. Perhaps Nate had Clara's cheque for $850,000.

He wondered what Nate would do when Fiona gave him the message to call. Try to explain? Stay away from him? Or go to the bank and get the money with Clara's cheque? If he did that, Sandy would know immediately and he would go to court to try to get it back.

But none of these things had happened yet. All he could do was wait.

Chapter 6   Wunderkind

John's new lawyer, Mel Tooley, phoned Sandy a few days later to discuss the subpoena and to find out any new information Sandy might have.

'I suppose they believe that Dixon's orders went to John,' said Sandy.

'Did they?' asked Mel.

'Possibly, but John does a very busy job and it's also possible he might not remember. I don't know if that's what happened, but it could be. What exactly does Ms Klonsky want with him?'

'I haven't talked to Sonia, just a few words with Stan,' replied Mel.

Stan Sennett was Sonia's boss and it seemed he was personally very interested in Dixon's problems.

Mel continued, 'I think John may be immune, if he tells them what they want to hear. Don't worry, Sandy, he's a nice young man – he'll be OK.'

Sandy guessed Mel's plan. It was that John should tell the government lawyers everything he knew, or thought he knew, about Dixon. In return, the government promised not to prosecute John. It was going to be one member of Sandy's family against another in court and it wasn't an idea he liked.

♦

The day of Margy's court appearance came. She had flown in from Chicago the night before and was in Sandy's office early the next morning. While they had coffee Sandy explained what was going to happen.

First, they were going to look at the papers together and try to think of the questions Ms Klonsky might ask. Then Margy and Sandy had to see Ms Klonsky in private. After that Margy had to go into court.

Sandy and Margy started examining the papers. Last on the government subpoena were the papers for the Wunderkind account.

'See what's strange about these?' said Margy, pointing at the figures.

'It looks as if he lost money.'

'He lost everything. But that's not all, look here.' Margy turned

29

to the last page. 'He kept losing until he had a deficit of a little more than $250,000.'

'Was the deficit paid off?'

'That's what it says here, but I didn't know anything about it.'

Sandy knew it was strange that Margy didn't know about a figure as large as $250,000.

'This can't be right,' said Sandy. 'Dixon's too clever to lose like that.'

'There's more bad news,' said Margy. She pointed to the subpoena.

'They want to see all the account details – names, addresses, who signed the papers. Well, we haven't got them. I can't find anything, not one paper, and there's nothing on the computer either. Everything has gone.'

Sandy could see now that things were looking very bad for Dixon. Today he already knew the end of the story. Dixon was going to prison.

♦

Together Sandy and Margy went to see Sonia Klonsky. She asked some questions and checked that all the papers were there. When she asked for the Wunderkind account details Sandy spoke.

'There's been a mistake somewhere. I'm sure someone has put the papers in the wrong place because Ms Allison can't find them. We'll continue to look, of course.'

Sonia wasn't happy, but it was time to go to court.

'I'll have to talk to Stan about this,' she said.

Margy and Sonia went into court. Sandy had to wait outside.

When Margy came out again he took her to a small room where they could talk. Then, after Margy had left to go back to Chicago, he saw Sonia again.

'I was looking for you Sandy. Stan wanted me to give you a message.'

'I was as annoyed as you that those papers were not there.'

'That's why I was talking to Stan. His message is this. Find Hartnell's safe.'

Sandy was shocked. They seemed to know everything. Perhaps it wasn't an informant but a hidden camera or microphone. He smiled at Sonia.

'Can you give me fifteen minutes of your time? I need to know a little more . . .'

'I can't do that, Sandy. Stan is really serious about this – I can't tell you any more.'

'Let me tell you what I think you know. You can just say if I'm right or wrong.'

Sonia thought about it.

'I really don't have the time. I have to finish work early today because I'm going away with my husband's son for the weekend. I've got a lot to do before I can go.'

'Let me come there, Saturday afternoon. Just fifteen minutes is all I need, Sonia.'

She laughed and gave him the address.

'If it's really that important to you. But I won't answer your questions, you know,' she said.

♦

Sandy phoned Dixon's home and talked first to Silvia, then to Dixon. He told him what had happened.

'There are a lot of problems we need to discuss, Dixon. They know about your safe.'

'How did they find out about that?' he asked.

'And some papers have disappeared. The Wunderkind account. Do you know about that?'

Sandy heard Dixon call to Silvia.

'I've got to go, your sister wants me. We'll talk about it next week. I'll be back on the 6th.'

'I have a lot of questions, Dixon, and you had better have the answers for me.'

Dixon called again to Silvia, then said goodbye to Sandy.

◆

Helen and Sandy had arranged to go out together on Saturday but he phoned her in the morning to say he had to drive out of town.

'I'll come with you,' said Helen.

'No, I'm sorry Helen but I have to see another lawyer about Dixon.'

'On Saturday?' Helen wasn't happy and Sandy felt she didn't believe him. They argued and in the end Helen put the phone down.

Sandy looked out of his window to Nate's house. He hadn't seen either him or Fiona. Once or twice he'd heard Nate's car as he came home late at night, but that was all. It looked as if Nate was keeping away from him.

On Saturday afternoon Sandy drove out of town to see Sonia. She was staying in the countryside at the house where her husband's parents had lived when they were alive.

Sandy found the house and arrived just as Sonia and her husband's son, Sam, were going to pick apples. So the three of them went together.

Outside the house, where the fields joined the garden, Sam started to run around and Sandy had a chance to talk to Sonia. Before he could start Sonia spoke.

'Stan is being very difficult about you and what he'll let you know. I don't think it's right, but I can't say too much. It's difficult for me. Do you understand?'

Sandy started telling her what he knew about Wunderkind and that the government had to be able to show the account was Dixon's to prosecute him.

'Go on,' she said, to show him he was right.

'Stan is being very difficult about you and what he'll let you know.'

'But those details have disappeared so you can't find the proof. Is this why you want John?' he asked.

'I really don't know about John. That subpoena came from Stan. But you've forgotten something.'

He thought for a moment.

'The deficit?'

'Go on,' she said again.

'If the government can show that Dixon paid the deficit they can prosecute. That's all the proof they need that Wunderkind is his account.'

'Go on.'

'And you have his cheque from the bank?'

Sonia nodded. But she couldn't tell him why Stan still needed John. Sandy didn't ask her any more.

'Nobody will ever know we had this conversation,' he promised. 'You have told me nothing.'

Then Sam came back, and they went together to pick apples.

Chapter 7   Another Lawyer

Monday was a day of surprises for Sandy.

First, Mel Tooley phoned him with some news about John.

'He's going to court next week. But I got this in private from Stan Sennett so keep it quiet.'

'Is John immune from prosecution?' asked Sandy.

Mel said yes, but the future for Dixon looked bad.

'John says Hartnell gave him all those orders and he remembers it clearly. He isn't happy about doing this, Sandy, since it's family. But I told him he must think of himself first.'

Sandy thought about what advice he should give Dixon now. He could lose everything, the house, his business and he might still have to go to prison. If that happened it would be awful for Silvia and

Sandy felt very sorry for her. He wondered how his family could ever be happy together again. It seemed impossible.

The second surprise came soon after. Sonia arrived in Sandy's office.

'How pleasant to see you again, Sonia,' he said, then stopped because Sonia wasn't smiling. She was holding a long white envelope.

'I came to give you this. I wanted to do it myself.'

He opened the envelope and read the paper inside. It was an FBI subpoena, addressed to Sandy personally. He had to appear in court the next Thursday, with Dixon's safe and all the papers contained in it.

Sonia was angry with him.

'You had those papers all the time. You said you would continue looking for them and they were in your office all the time. You lied to me Sandy, and I thought you were my friend.'

'I am your friend. I don't know what is in the safe.'

'I know you have to do your job, but you're making things difficult for me with Stan. You must be in court on Thursday with the safe.'

'I can't do that unless Mr Hartnell agrees and he's out of town until late Thursday.'

'Then you'd better get a lawyer, Sandy.'

Sonia opened the door.

'You're going to need a good lawyer,' she said.

At the same moment, Marta appeared behind her. Sandy was surprised to see her because he had forgotten she was coming home for a week.

'Who needs a lawyer?' asked Marta and Sandy showed her the subpoena.

He decided to take Marta out for dinner and they found a quiet restaurant where they could talk.

They discussed Kate. Marta said she was tired and that she was worried about John.

They looked again at the subpoena.

'Sonia's right. I will need a lawyer.'

'I could do it,' said Marta, 'if you helped me.'

Sandy thought about it. Marta was a good lawyer, perhaps the best person to advise him in court because she already knew most of the details. Anyway, he thought, it kept it in the family.

'Very well, Marta. You can have the job.'

◆

On Wednesday morning Marta went to work with Sandy. She looked at the safe which was standing behind his desk.

'Is that it? And you've never opened it?'

'I haven't got the key and your uncle has never said I could anyway. He likes to be private.'

Marta was a clever lawyer and she could see a problem with Sandy's subpoena.

'When you go to court you'll have to say the contents of the safe were here in your office so that you could advise Dixon about them. But how can we say that, if you've never seen what's inside?'

They discussed the problem together. In the end they decided Sandy should tell the court that he couldn't say anything more until he had spoken to Dixon again.

'What happens if the judge orders you to speak about the contents tomorrow?' asked Marta.

'I must refuse.'

'And can they put you in prison?'

'Not tomorrow. They'll give me time to think again. After that, I am in your hands.'

Marta kissed him.

'No problem. Just be sure to bring your toothbrush,' she said.

◆

On Thursday morning at ten o'clock they were all there –
Sandy, Marta, Sonia and the judge. Her name was Moira Winchell
and she was someone Sandy had known for years. Soon after ten
Sonia's boss, Stan Sennett, arrived.

In the court everything happened very quickly. Finally the judge
decided the court would let Sandy have time to speak to Dixon and
another date was arranged, for two weeks' time.

Marta told her father she didn't have much work in New York
and she could come back to Kindle before the date for the next
court appearance. Sandy agreed to this, but he had already decided
that if Dixon didn't give the papers to the court he would not
continue as his lawyer.

♦

By five o'clock that evening he still hadn't heard from Dixon. He
had phoned his secretary twice and then Silvia. She promised she
would ask her husband to phone Sandy as soon as he arrived home.

Late in the day he returned to his empty office to look at
some papers and was surprised to see Dixon already there. He had
forgotten he had given him a key.

'Silvia says you're not seeing Helen any more,' he said. 'That's a
pity – she's an interesting lady.'

'And you, Dixon, are a difficult man. We have to talk seriously now.'

Dixon looked at his watch.

'I've got ten minutes then I have to go to the airport.'

'You're going to prison, Dixon.'

'No I'm not. That's why I pay you.'

'I can't change the proof.'

Dixon took another cigarette from a packet.

'You want me to say I'm guilty?'

Sandy nodded yes, and told him about John.

'He's going to court next week and he will tell them he did what
you told him to do. You can't blame him for that, Dixon. He's a

young man and his wife's going to have a baby. If he does this, he'll be immune from prosecution.'

Dixon looked worried when he heard that.

'They still need proof that I made a profit and they won't have that without those Wunderkind papers.

Sandy pointed to the safe behind his desk.

'I believe they have found them.'

He showed him the subpoena he had received.

'You said my things would be safe if I brought them here,' said Dixon.

'I said your personal things, but these are company papers.

Dixon took off his jacket and picked up the safe. It was very heavy and it was difficult for him to walk a few steps with it.

'You can't take the safe away, Dixon. The subpoena is addressed to me and I have to have the safe in court next time I appear. If not, they could put me in prison.'

Dixon put the safe down.

'They won't do that. They all think you're wonderful.'

He picked the safe up again and walked very slowly towards the door with it.

'Then I cannot be your lawyer any more.'

Dixon was near the door and he stopped to look back at Sandy.

'Then I'll find another.'

Sandy picked up the telephone.

'Taking that safe from here is a crime. If you do it, I'll have to phone the FBI.'

Dixon waited for a moment.

'I'm not joking, Dixon. I mean what I say.'

Sandy spoke into the telephone but as he did so Dixon put the safe down just inside the door. His face was red and it was difficult for him to breathe. He came back into the room and as Sandy put the phone down he picked up his jacket and left without a word.

'Taking that safe from here is a crime. If you do it, I'll have to phone the FBI.'

Chapter 8   The Safe

On the evening Marta was flying back to New York Sandy met her and Kate for dinner. Peter couldn't come because he was working at the hospital. Sandy asked Kate where John was.

'He's with his lawyer,' she said. He could see that Kate was very worried about John's court appearance.

'This problem with your uncle – you must tell John he's not to blame for anything that has happened,' he told her.

When they left the restaurant Kate drove home and Sandy took Marta to the airport. After that he went back to his house. Nate and Fiona's house was completely dark, like his. He still hadn't seen Nate and knew that soon he must find a way to talk to him.

Inside the quiet, empty house Sandy realized that although he was sad and often lonely, his life had moved on without Clara. He thought suddenly of Helen, and felt very sorry that they had argued. He decided to try to see her again. That night he slept well and was up by six o'clock. By seven he was in the office, as he had always been before Clara had died.

It took him more than an hour to notice that something was different. Dixon's safe had gone.

◆

'This isn't funny,' said Marta on the telephone from New York. 'You've got to get it back. If you appear in court without it they could put you in prison.'

Sandy tried all weekend to speak to Dixon. Finally, on Monday, he got through to him.

'Someone has stolen it,' said Dixon. 'Call the police. There are important papers in there.'

Sandy was very angry. He was certain Dixon had taken the safe but he continued to deny it.

On Wednesday, when Sandy was talking to Silvia, he said something about the safe.

'Oh, that thing,' she replied. 'It's here. It arrived in the middle of the night, Dixon and our driver carried it in.'

She told Sandy the sound of the two men arguing had woken her up. Dixon wouldn't let the driver carry the safe alone but Silvia could see that it was very heavy. Lifting it had made Dixon quite ill and it was difficult for him to breathe.

'They took it as far as the living-room and it's still there now.'

'I think I may come to see you Silvia. Tomorrow, if that's all right?'

◆

Later that day Sonia phoned Sandy because she needed Marta's phone number in New York. It was a week before Sandy had to appear in court.

'We've thought about that again,' said Sonia. 'Just deliver the safe and sign a paper to say everything is still in it. If you do that, you won't have to appear in court.'

Sandy didn't tell her that Dixon had the safe again. But he sent a message to Dixon. It said that unless he returned the safe before another two days Sandy could not be his lawyer any more.

◆

When he drove home that evening Sandy saw Nate working in his garden. As he got out of his car, Nate walked towards him.

'I think we should talk,' said Nate. 'Maybe have a drink together. I have to apologize to you, Sandy.'

They went into Sandy's house.

'I know Fiona found the pills and showed them to you. It was wrong of me not to tell you, Sandy. I'm sorry.'

'If they were Clara's pills, why did you keep them?'

'She wouldn't have them in the house, she was afraid you might

41

find them. I came in each morning to give her the correct number for that day. I was wrong to lie to you about the Westlab test but I was very worried.'

'That I might find out Clara had herpes?'

Nate shook his head.

'I was afraid you might sue me. You're a lawyer and it would be easy for you if you wanted to take me to court.'

Sandy didn't understand.

'Why did you think I might sue you Nate?'

'I blame myself for Clara's death. She had talked about killing herself before, whenever the herpes returned. As her doctor, it was my job to stay here to watch her but instead I went away to Montreal for a weekend.'

Sandy had sat down. Nate was saying strange things.

'How long had Clara had herpes?'

'About seven years. It returned occasionally but the last time was the worst. That's why she had another test. The pills weren't helping and she was very unhappy. But I didn't realize how unhappy she was, so I didn't look after her as well as I should have done. I gave her all the pills she needed for the weekend and I went away.'

Sandy was shocked. Seven years. Nate continued.

'I had talked to another doctor and told him the whole story. I hoped he would watch Clara during the weekend.'

Sandy looked up at Nate.

'You need not worry, Nate, I won't sue you. You did what you thought was best for Clara. As her doctor, you had to keep her secret.'

They walked to the door together. Nate shook hands with Sandy, then he said, 'I don't know who the man was, Sandy. But she told me it had only happened once. The most important thing to her was that you wouldn't find out.'

Sandy nodded and closed the door on Nate. He still hadn't got the answers he wanted.

◆

University of Winchester
Tel: 01962 827306
E-Mail: libenquiries@winchester.ac.uk

Borrowed items 19/09/2014 11:45

XXXX4607

Item Title	Due Date
* burden of proof	17/10/2014
* diary of a young girl	17/10/2014
Media studies	16/10/2014
Academic encounters : reading, study skills, and writing : content focus, hu	16/10/2014

* indicates items borrowed today
Thankyou for using this unit

Next day, Sandy drove to Silvia and Dixon's house. It was a big, expensive house outside the town and had an enormous garden with a swimming pool.

Inside, while Silvia made them coffee, they talked about Dixon.

'You must tell me what is happening,' said Silvia. 'Dixon says nothing, but I know he's worried. Is it serious?'

'Very.'

Sandy explained a little about the government lawyers and told Silvia that they needed the safe and the papers inside it.

'Is he in danger of going to prison?'

'Yes, he is.'

Silvia gave Sandy his coffee and they sat together in her kitchen.

'I'm worried about him, Sandy. I think he's ill. Every morning he coughs badly for half an hour. He forgets everything. He doesn't sleep and sometimes goes out in the middle of the night. Last week he didn't sleep here once.'

Sandy felt very sorry for his sister.

'Have you asked him where he goes?'

'To the office, he says, but when I phone there's no reply.'

'I hope you won't have to separate again,' said Sandy, remembering the time years before when Silvia had made Dixon leave the house.

'Yes. I suppose Clara told you all about that? About the . . . the virus?'

Sandy felt himself go cold. He asked Silvia to explain.

'Dixon had caught a terrible virus. I was worried I might have it too, but I was lucky.'

'What was it, this virus?' he asked, but he knew the answer already.

'It was herpes,' she replied.

◆

Silvia's phone rang and while she answered it Sandy went into the

At the end of the second page the same person had signed.
Her name was Kate Stern.

living-room. As he walked in he saw Dixon's safe on the floor behind the sofa. He touched it with the toe of his shoe and the door opened just a little. Dixon hadn't locked it.

He could hear Silvia's voice on the phone in the kitchen. He took the papers out of the safe. As he opened them flat he saw a cheque. It was for $850,000, written to Dixon Hartnell and signed by Clara Stern.

He looked at the papers. They were the information papers for the Wunderkind account. The first page showed the name and address of the person who the account belonged to. At the end of the second page the same person had signed. Her name was Kate Stern.

Chapter 9   Some Answers

Next day, Sandy phoned Clara's lawyer, to say he had found the cheque. He didn't tell him the details, just that he had solved the problem.

When he returned home that evening, Marta was there.

'I've left my job,' she said. 'I decided to come back home and work here in Kindle. It will be nice to be able to help Kate when the baby's born.'

They talked about John's appearance that day in court.

'He blamed everything on your uncle,' said Sandy. 'He said Dixon gave him the orders and he didn't understand what was happening because he was new in the job.'

'And Dixon's safe?'

'I haven't got it.'

'We must tell Judge Winchell you're not going to be his lawyer any more.'

'I'll still have to appear in court.'

They decided they should spend the next day planning what they would say in court.

◆

On Tuesday morning Sandy arrived at his office before seven o'clock. When he walked into his room he was surprised to see Dixon asleep on the sofa. Next to him on the floor was the safe. When the phone rang a little later Dixon woke up.

'I've brought you the safe. That will solve your problems.'

'I have to say nothing was taken from it, Dixon. How can I do that?'

Dixon opened the safe and gave him the only piece of paper in there. It was his cheque for $250,000. It was the proof that he had paid the Wunderkind deficit.

'They already have a copy of this from your bank, Dixon. What they want are the Wunderkind account details.'

'I haven't got them. I'll just say I'm guilty. That was your advice last time we talked. If I do that, what will the courts do?'

'You'll lose MD and have to pay a lot of money. And you'll go to prison, probably for about three years. But I can't understand why you're doing this.'

'Because I'm guilty, I told you. I stole the money, put it in the house error account and then hid it in the Wunderkind account. I cheated the markets.'

Sandy shook his head.

'You're lying Dixon.'

Dixon lit another cigarette and walked across Sandy's office to the window.

'That account, Wunderkind. I wanted it to be John's account. I asked him to open it because I knew I couldn't. We couldn't use his name though, so Kate signed with her unmarried name.'

'And John didn't get any profit?'

'Nothing. There wasn't anything, remember? I lost it all.'

'I believe there's more to tell than that. I don't think you're so stupid. You might be guilty of other crimes but I don't think you're guilty of this one.'

46

Dixon became very angry and for a moment Sandy thought he might hit him.

Dixon became very angry and for a moment Sandy thought he might hit him.

'I'll get another lawyer. I don't need you.' Then he walked out.

♦

Peter had phoned Sandy the day before to say that he had the test results. It was good news, Sandy didn't have herpes. After Dixon left the office, Sandy decided to go and see Peter. He was a little worried about Kate's health because she looked so tired all the time. Peter had a day's holiday so Sandy drove across town to his flat.

Peter looked surprised to see him.

'Why didn't you call?' he asked.

'Are you busy?'

Sandy walked into the living-room with Peter.

'There's somebody here, Dad. I have a guest.'

There was the sound of a cough from the bedroom. It was obviously a man. Sandy felt embarrassed.

'We'll talk some other time,' he said and as he turned to the door he saw the man's jacket on the sofa. He knew he had seen it before but couldn't remember when or where. Peter led him to the door and opened it but suddenly Sandy remembered. He went back into the room to look again.

'You'd better come out,' he said.

The bedroom door opened and the man who came out was the FBI detective who had given Dixon his subpoena on the day of Clara's funeral. Then he understood.

'I believe you have used my son as your informant. The nephew of the man you were trying to prosecute. That can't be right.'

'Everything's been done correctly, you'll see,' he said to Sandy. Then he took his jacket and left.

Peter sat down.

'Let me explain, Dad. It was the right thing to do and I'm not sorry. About six weeks before Mum died, Kate came to see me.

She had just found out about the baby and she wanted to ask me about having an abortion. She said it was because John had done something really stupid at MD and they were afraid he was in big trouble.'

Sandy sat on the sofa opposite Peter, afraid of what he was going to hear next.

'They had decided John could make some money if he opened an account at MD and put in his own orders. He wanted to show us all that he could succeed and they needed the extra money. Kate signed the papers and before long he started to make a profit. He knew how to use the house error account to hide what he was doing and he knew it wasn't right but he thought "Just one more time".'

'And that's when it went wrong?'

'Yes. John was buying sugar and suddenly the price of sugar fell. He lost everything he'd stolen, and more. John didn't know what to do. He took all the papers about Wunderkind and burned them. He made certain there was nothing left on the computer. Then he called someone he knows in the Chicago office and asked him to send the copy papers. But this man spoke to Dixon about it first.'

'Dixon paid the deficit himself.'

'Yes, but only after he'd hit John and hurt him badly. Then he told him he was going to talk to the FBI. John was really frightened. Dixon kept saying, "I'm going tomorrow" and he made John do all the dirty jobs around the office. He told John he was keeping the papers in his personal safe until he gave them to the FBI.'

'And John believed him.'

'So when Kate came to see me they had decided John should go to the FBI himself and say he was guilty. If he did that, he would go to prison. That was why Kate wanted an abortion.'

'And you?' asked Sandy.

'I thought about it and realized what John must do. Go to the

FBI, yes. But blame Dixon for Wunderkind and say that John was just doing what Dixon told him.'

'And you were working between John and the FBI?'

'Yes. I was Stan Sennett's informant. He promised not to prosecute John in return for what I told him.'

'Do you think it was right to do this to your uncle for what he did to John?'

Peter looked uncomfortable.

'It wasn't only for that. Dixon has done other terrible things in his life.' He was quiet for a moment.

'Nate told me he talked to you about Mum the other day. I was the other doctor he spoke to before he went to Montreal, that weekend when she died. He thinks he made a serious mistake. Remember, I was Dixon's doctor, too. I checked his details and found that he had had herpes, too. A long time before.'

Sandy waited for a moment before he asked Peter about Clara.

'Why did you tell your mother about this?'

'I had to. She could see how worried Kate was and eventually Kate told her about John's problems at MD. She said I was helping them. So then Mum asked me and I told her the plan.'

Sandy stood up and started to walk to the door.

'Peter, what you have done is completely wrong. Our whole family may be broken by this.'

Peter nodded.

'That's what Mum thought. She was very shocked and frightened for all of us. I think it was the thing that made her finally decide to kill herself.'

As they said goodbye at the door, Peter asked, 'What's going to happen now, Dad? Is there anything you can do?'

But Sandy just shook his head. At that moment he had no ideas at all.

Chapter 10   Second Chances

Dixon was asleep on Sandy's sofa again the next morning when he arrived at the office. When he woke up he immediately lit a cigarette.

'I'm surprised to see you here,' said Sandy. 'I thought you wanted another lawyer.'

'I changed my mind. Anyway, I'm family.'

'I would like you to tell me about Clara's cheque. She paid you $850,000 – the figure her daughter's husband stole and lost on the Wunderkind account. But you kept her cheque and paid the Wunderkind deficit yourself.'

Dixon started walking up and down Sandy's office.

'So, you know about that. Clara knew John and I were both in trouble and she thought I might take all the blame myself. The $850,000 was to pay for the costs.'

'That's a lie!' Sandy hit the top of his desk.

'I know about everything, Dixon. I know that you decided to pay the deficit and then punish John yourself. And because of this, you were informed against.'

Dixon went back to the sofa and sat down.

'John was very frightened of you talking to the FBI. He thought you meant it,' continued Sandy.

'I didn't know about the baby.'

'If you knew, would it have been different?'

'Maybe.'

'When was the last time you saw Clara?'

'Three, four days before she died. She gave me the cheque to pay for John's mistakes. I told her I didn't want it and threw it in the safe. That's the whole story.'

Sandy shook his head. There was more to the story and he wanted to make Dixon tell him everything.

'But you changed your mind. At first you wanted to hand John to the FBI, then suddenly you decided not to do it and started taking the blame yourself. Why did you do that Dixon?'

Dixon's face told Sandy nothing. He sat silently on the sofa, smoking his cigarette.

'And what about my wife? Shall we talk about Clara? And shall we discuss your sex life and herpes?'

Dixon stood up and walked round the office.

'I can't explain. It only happened once and it was a long time ago. You were working in Kansas. Kate had just gone away to university and it was a bad time for Clara. I was to blame completely. And it didn't mean anything. If she hadn't caught herpes, you could have said nothing happened.'

Sandy sat at his desk and watched Dixon.

'Then, when I realized about the herpes, I told Silvia she had to be examined and she threw me out of the house. And went to cry on Clara's shoulder.'

'And the last time you saw Clara?'

Dixon had sat down again. He sat opposite Sandy, but he wasn't looking at him.

'She came to my office, sat down and cried. Told me everything about John, Peter and the doctors. Then she gave me the money. She thought it would all be all right if she paid. She just wanted her children to be safe.'

'And how did the conversation end?'

'She was afraid she might have to tell you about the herpes because the doctors couldn't control it. Then she said "I'm not certain that I can go on." It was the most frightening moment of my life. I tried to tell her Peter and John and Kate were going to be OK. And I promised her. I said I would take the blame for everything John had done, if it went to court. I was sorry for her, and sorry for what I'd done.'

'But you're innocent, Dixon. Peter and John chose to do what they did.'

Dixon looked for a moment as if he might cry.

'They're children. I promised Clara. Just let me say I'm guilty and pay for it. Prison won't be so bad.'

Sandy came and sat next to Dixon.

'I can't let you. I'm still your lawyer.'

'Forget that. You've got to let me do this. They're your children.'

Eventually, Sandy saw that Dixon was right. It was still early but they decided to phone the government lawyers' office at once. They were lucky. Stan Sennett was at work early and answered the phone himself.

♦

When the telephone rang Sandy was dreaming. He switched on the light and saw that the time was 3 a.m.

He answered the phone and heard Helen's voice.

'I need you,' she said. 'I'm sorry, I need you here.' She kept repeating that she was sorry. Something was obviously wrong and Sandy got up at once and dressed. As he drove to Helen's house he wondered if there was a problem with one of her children.

When he arrived he saw an ambulance outside Helen's garage.

'Not again,' he thought. 'God, not again.'

Helen was waiting by the door and opened it as soon as he got there. She was crying and her make-up had run down her face. He put his arms around her and realized how much he loved her.

'What is it?'

'Sandy, I'm sorry. I had to call you. You were the only person I could think of . . .'

An ambulance man appeared at the top of the stairs. He called to them and then shook his head.

'It's no good, he's dead,' he said.

Sandy went upstairs and followed him to Helen's bedroom.

There was a man on her bed. He had no clothes on and his head was turned away from the door, but already Sandy knew.

'His heart,' said the ambulance man.

Helen came up behind Sandy and he turned to her.

'Oh my God. Helen, tell me that isn't Dixon.'

But she just shook her head.

The ambulance man told them he had to phone the police, but Sandy asked if he could do it. He called Ray Radczyk and explained what had happened.

'I need your help,' he said.

While they waited for Radczyk to arrive Sandy and Helen sat together in her living-room.

'I'm sorry I had to call,' she said again.

'When did this start, with Dixon?' he asked.

'I was very sad, after we argued. Dixon called me the same week and I enjoyed being with him.'

It explained where Dixon had been at nights when he wasn't at home with Silvia. They sat silently until they saw the lights of a car outside.

Sandy opened the door to Radczyk. Helen told him her story in as few words as possible. They had been in bed together, he had suddenly become ill.

Radczyk took Sandy away from the living-room where Helen was sitting.

'Am I right to think he wasn't that lady's husband?'

'Ms Dudak is single. He was my sister's husband. This will be a terrible shock for her.'

'OK, I understand. Now, what do you want to do?'

Sandy explained and together they went upstairs. Radczyk checked Dixon's body to make certain his death was natural. He spoke to the ambulance men who told him they had tested Dixon's heart. Then he sent them away.

'There's no problem here, Sandy. I've got to make a few calls first, though. Get the computer information changed, you understand?'

When he came back from the telephone they dressed Dixon's

When he came back from the telephone they dressed Dixon's body and carried it down to Sandy's car.

body and carried it down to Sandy's car. Sandy explained to Helen what they were going to do.

'It'll be easier for Silvia this way,' he said.

Helen nodded.

He told her about Dixon and Clara, and realized then that there was nothing he couldn't say to Helen. So he told her a little more about what John, Kate and Peter had done. He knew that Helen and he were not going to have any secrets from each other in the future and in that moment he was certain he wanted to marry her.

'Do you think we go through life making the same mistakes?' she asked him.

'It can happen.' He took her hand in his. 'But I also believe in second chances.'

'I feel that, too,' she said.

◆

Sandy drove across town to his office with Dixon's body on the back seat. Behind him Radczyk drove his car. When they arrived, they carried the body in through the back door and went up in the lift to Sandy's room.

They put Dixon's body on the sofa, just as Sandy had found him on several mornings recently.

'How can I thank you?' asked Sandy.

'There's no need. It's better this way.'

After Radczyk had gone, Sandy sat alone in his office with Dixon and, as he looked at him, he cried.

◆

On the back of his door was an extra suit and in his desk a clean shirt and tie. He changed into these clothes and it looked as if he had arrived at the office as usual, ready for work. As soon as he heard the first sounds of someone coming into the building he intended to phone Silvia. He planned to say he had just come to the office and found Dixon on his sofa where he had spent many recent nights.

He looked at the photos on his desk of his family. The children were now completely free. With Dixon's death the government could not continue investigating his business. It was all over.

And with Clara's money, they were rich. They were all going to have their second chances, too.

He tried to imagine how it might be for the family in the future. It was going to be difficult for them to be a happy family again. But then he remembered – there was going to be a baby. The child might bring them all together again as new people – parents, grandfather, aunts, uncle. The future didn't seem so bad.

Downstairs, Sandy heard someone arriving for work and he picked up the telephone to call Silvia.

'Something terrible,' he told her. She knew at once.

'We'll manage it together,' he said 'I can help. The family will help.'

ACTIVITIES

Chapters 1–2

Before you read

1 Look at the picture on page 3. How would you describe the mood of the two men in the picture? What do you think connects them?

2 Check these words in your dictionary:

account error investigate profit proof

Choose the right word for each sentence.

  a Detectives or lawyers do this when they ask a lot of questions about somebody.

  b Another word for a mistake.

  c You have one of these at a bank to keep a check on how much money you have.

  d You will make this if you sell something for more than you buy it for.

  e The police might think someone is a criminal but they must have this before they can be certain.

3 Now look at these words:

burden funeral prosecute safe (n) *subpoena*

Put the correct words into these sentences.

  a You can keep your money locked up in a . . . . . in the bank.

  b The family of the dead woman were all at her . . . . . .

  c Something heavy or difficult to carry is a . . . . . .

  d The police gave him a . . . . . and the lawyer said he must obey it.

  e The police talked to a lot of witnesses and then decided to . . . . . her for the murder.

After you read

4 When you get married, your husband or wife's family become your *in-laws*. What is the relationship between these people?

  a Peter is Dixon's . . . . .   d Marta is Silvia's . . . . .

  b Dixon is Kate's . . . . .   e John is Peter's . . . . .

  c Sandy is John's . . . . .

5 What are the two surprises for the family on the day of the funeral?

6 Why does MD have a house error account?

Chapters 3–4

Before you read

7 What do you think Clara wanted $850,000 for?

8 Check these words in your dictionary, then put the correct word in each sentence:

herpes immune virus

  a The doctor gave her some pills to take for ......

  b 'You might not get the disease. Some people are ......'

  c 'She is suffering from a ..... but the doctor doesn't know exactly what it is.'

After you read

9 *Student A*: You are Ray Radczyk.

  Student B: You work at the Westlab Hospital.

  Act your conversation at the hospital (pages 16 and 17).

10 Dixon is making a profit from cheating the markets. What does Margy think Dixon is doing with the money?

11 What does Ms Fiori remember about Clara's cheque for $850,000?

Chapters 5–6

Before you read

12 Check the word *deficit* in your dictionary.

  Make a sentence using this group of words:

  account/deficit/paid

13 What do you think Dixon almost said to Sandy at lunch?

After you read

14 Who says these things? Who to?

  a 'There are some good things about being alone again.'

  b 'I'll find all the details by the 27th.'

  c 'I'm sorry I haven't called you but I've been very busy.'

Chapters 7–8

Before you read

15 Check the verb *sue* in your dictionary, then write a sentence using these words: doctor/sue/court/judge

59

16 Where do you think the Wunderkind papers are?

After you read

17 Where did these things happen?
  a Sonia gives Sandy an FBI subpoena.
  b Marta offers to be Sandy's lawyer.
  c Nate tells Sandy about Clara's pills.

Chapters 9–10

Before you read

18 Find the word *abortion* in your dictionary. In this story, who do you think had, or wanted, an abortion?

19 Clara gave the $850,000 cheque to Dixon, but why do you think he hasn't cashed it?

After you read

20 What is in the safe when Dixon returns it?

21 Why has Peter become the government's informant?

22 Why does Dixon say he is guilty if it isn't true?

23 What do Sandy and Radczyk do with Dixon's body?

Writing

24 Sonia, Margy, Peter and Radczyk have very different jobs. Whose job do you think is the most interesting, and why?

25 Imagine you are at a family party at Sandy's house a year after this book ends. Write a description. Say who is there and describe how life has changed for the Stern family.

26 Write a report for the *Kindle County Newspaper* explaining Dixon's death and telling readers a little about his business.

27 Which are the good characters and which are the bad ones in this story? Are any of the characters 'black' or 'white', or are they all a mixture of good and bad? Write a paragraph with your ideas.

Answers for the Activities in this book are published in our free resource packs for teachers, the Penguin Readers Factsheets, or available on a separate sheet. Please write to your local Pearson Education office or to: Marketing Department, Penguin Longman Publishing, 5 Bentinck Street, London W1M 5RN.